PEANUTS®

Snoopy and Woodstock's Great Adventure

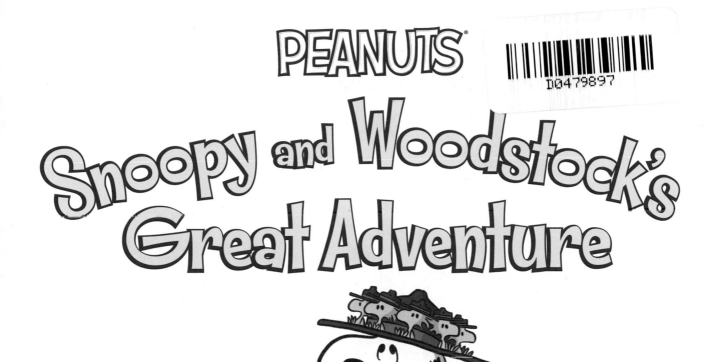

By Charles M. Schulz

Adapted by Lauren Forte
Illustrated by Scott Jeralds

SIMON SPOTLIGHT
New York   London   Toronto   Sydney   New Delhi

SIMON SPOTLIGHT
An imprint of Simon & Schuster Children's Publishing Division
1230 Avenue of the Americas, New York, New York 10020
First Simon Spotlight edition December 2015
© 2015 Peanuts Worldwide LLC
SIMON SPOTLIGHT and colophon are registered trademarks of Simon & Schuster, Inc.
For information about special discounts for bulk purchases, please contact Simon & Schuster
Special Sales at 1-866-506-1949 or business@simonandschuster.com.
Manufactured in the United States of America 1115 LAK
10 9 8 7 6 5 4 3 2 1
ISBN 978-1-4814-5196-3
ISBN 978-1-4814-5197-0 (eBook)

This is Snoopy. And these are his friends Conrad, Olivier, Bill, Harriet, and Woodstock.

It is such a beautiful day that Snoopy, the world-famous Beagle Scout, is leading his troops out into the wilderness.

"Charlie Brown, I just saw your dog go by. Where is he going?" Lucy asks.
"He's taking his friends to Point Lobos on a photo hike," he answers.

"Point Lobos?" Lucy responds. "Doesn't he know how far that is? How's he ever going to find it?"
Charlie Brown is not worried. Snoopy goes on adventures all the time.

"All right, troops," Snoopy calls out. "Let's have an equipment check. Bill, what did you bring?"

Bill chirps excitedly.

"A compass?" Snoopy says, surprised. "You think we're going to get lost? Woodstock, what did you bring?"

Woodstock holds up some rain gear.

"Rain gear? Good grief. It isn't going to rain."

Snoopy rolls his eyes as he looks at the rest of the things they brought. He tosses aside a flashlight from Olivier and a first-aid kit from Conrad. His friends are such worriers!

"All right, Harriet, how about you?" Snoopy barks.

Harriet smiles and proudly holds up a plate.

"An angel food cake with seven-minute frosting?" Snoopy says, relieved. "Well, I'm glad we have at least one sensible hiker in our group!"

Before they set out, Snoopy makes sure all the scouts have their cameras.

"Good," he says. Snoopy gestures to the forest ahead of them. "Now on today's photo hike, you'll get to take some beautiful, and maybe unusual, pictures . . ."

But when Snoopy turns around, the scouts are just taking photos with each other! "Not of yourselves!" says Snoopy. He turns and leads the group onto the path with a sigh.

The hike begins! As they walk, they stop along the way to take pictures of fluffy clouds, tall trees, and oddly shaped rocks.

But as they reach some very overgrown weeds, Snoopy calls out a warning, "All right, troops. We're entering tall grass. This could mean queen snakes! We should walk single file—"

"Or . . . vertical file," Snoopy says under his breath, as the birds all perch on top of his hat.

Snoopy walks through the field warily, on the lookout for queen snakes!

Once they've cleared the tall grass, Snoopy lets the birds back down onto the path. Luckily they didn't run into any snakes, but now the ground is bumpy, and the scouts are getting tired. Hiking is hard work.

Olivier chirps a question.

"A walking stick?" asks Snoopy. "You're right. We all should have walking sticks."

Olivier volunteers to gather walking sticks for everyone.

But when Olivier returns with the sticks, there's just one problem: They're all bird-size!

This is not so helpful, thinks Snoopy as they continue along the trail.

"Can someone get up in a tree or something and try to see where we're going?" Snoopy asks a few hours later. They have to be close to Point Lobos by now!

Bill silently wonders if his compass would have been helpful after all. It's easy to get lost in the woods.

"Harriet?" Snoopy calls on her. "Get up as high as you can and tell us what you see."

Harriet flies up onto the brim of Snoopy's hat to get a good look around.

"Actually, Harriet, I was hoping you'd get up a little higher than that," Snoopy says sarcastically.

Still, Harriet sees the way! She chirps that they are on the right path—in fact, they're almost there!

As the friends head up the final hill, Snoopy has an idea.

"When we get to the top," Snoopy says while panting, "we'll eat the angel food cake that Harriet brought."

Bill and Olivier chirp in agreement—they've really worked up an appetite!

But then Conrad chirps back angrily.

"What?" Snoopy cries. "Why can't we eat the cake at the top of the hill?"

Conrad chirps again.

"Because Harriet ate it at the bottom of the hill!" repeats Snoopy. "Argh!"

But Snoopy can't stay mad at Harriet for long. As they round the top of the hill, they finally arrive at Point Lobos, and the view is spectacular.

Snoopy takes a deep breath and looks out over the water. "There it is, gang—the Pacific Ocean!"

The scouts stare at the scenery for a long time, thinking about how beautiful it looks, until Snoopy encourages them to get out their cameras.

"Now I want you to take a lot of pictures of what you see. That's what we're here for," Snoopy instructs as the birds start snapping away.

The scouts notice that there are colorful flowers growing all around the cliffs.

Snoopy points out a pretty purple one. Bill tries to take a picture of it, but there's a bee near the flower. It's buzzing and flitting all around, and Bill can't get a good shot!

"Be polite," Snoopy tells Bill. "Ask the bee if he minds moving."

This time it's Bill who rolls his eyes.

As the sun sets and it begins to get dark, the world-famous Beagle Scout and his troops set up camp for the night.

Of course no campout is complete without marshmallows. Conrad gets a tree branch and begins roasting them . . . all at once!

As the scouts get ready to settle in for the night, they munch on the huge pile of marshmallows and gaze at the starry sky.

"Look, there's a full moon tonight," Snoopy points out.

The birds are suddenly nervous and start chirping to Snoopy all at once.

"No. There aren't such things as werewolves. That's just a myth," Snoopy reassures them and continues. "But you know who really comes out when the moon is full?"

"The Werebeagle!" Snoopy shouts, making a scary face.
All the birds dive into their sleeping bags for cover!
Snoopy laughs and laughs.

"Okay, troops. It's bedtime," Snoopy says after everyone calms down. One by one the scouts hop onto Snoopy's sleeping bag and settle in for the night.

What a great day it was to hike with friends. Good night, Beagle Scouts!